W9-ASX-981

Disney PRESS
New York

TRIPLE-R

Andy raced around his room, playing with his two special toys. "You should never mess with the unstoppable duo of Sheriff Woody and Buzz Lightyear!" Andy said.

Suddenly, there was a loud *RIIIPPP*! Woody's shoulder had torn! Andy was supposed to leave for Cowboy Camp any minute and had to decide if he would still take Woody.

Andy's mother suggested they try to mend the cowboy, but Andy decided to leave him at home this year.

Woody sat on the shelf and watched sadly as Andy left. Andy had never gone to Cowboy Camp without him before. **Woody wondered if Andy would forget about him.** He didn't feel any better when he noticed Wheezy, a toy penguin who'd been sitting broken and forgotten on the shelf for months. Was that Woody's future, too?

After dropping off Andy at camp, Andy's mother began to set up for a yard sale. When she came up to Andy's room to find items for the sale, **she grabbed Wheezy off the shelf!**

Woody sprang into action. He jumped onto Andy's dog, Buster, to rescue the penguin. Wheezy made it back safely to Andy's room, but Woody had fallen off in the yard.

Soon, Woody was spotted by a stranger. The man picked up the toy cowboy and clutched him in his hands. "I found him!" he exclaimed. "How much for this stuff?" he asked Andy's mother.

Andy's mother refused to sell Woody, so the stranger stole him and ran off!

"Oh, no!" cried Buzz, watching from Andy's bedroom window. "He's stealing Woody!"

In a flash, Buzz leaped out the window and slid down the drainpipe.

But Buzz was too late. The stranger had jumped into his car with Woody and was speeding off. The last thing Buzz saw was the car's license plate, which read LZTYBRN.

The thief raced back to his home and put Woody in a glass case. Once the man left, Woody opened the case and escaped.

Suddenly, a packing box burst open and three unfamiliar toys surrounded Woody: a cowgirl, a horse, and a prospector still in his original box.

"Yee-haw! It's you! It's really you!" shouted the cowgirl.

The horse eagerly licked Woody's face.

"We've waited countless years for this day, Woody," the Prospector said, smiling.

"Who are you?" Woody asked, confused. **"How do you know my name?"**

Meanwhile, Buzz learned that the license plate LZTYBRN belonged to Al, the owner of Al's Toy Barn. The toys knew Al from his TV commercials. It was Al who had stolen Woody!

Buzz outlined a plan to get Woody back.

"Woody once risked his life to save me," Buzz explained. "I couldn't call myself his friend if I wasn't willing to do the same. Who's with me?" he asked.

Later that night, Buzz, Slinky Dog, Hamm, and Rex set out to rescue their stolen friend. Buzz led the way. **"To Al's Toy Barn—and beyond!"** he cried.

Back at Al's apartment, the toys introduced themselves: Jessie the yodeling cowgirl, Stinky Pete the Prospector, and Bullseye, the sharpest horse in the West.

Then the Prospector explained that they were part of a collection based on a TV show called *Woody's Roundup,* **and Woody was the star.**

Al had collected every toy from the show except for one—Sheriff Woody. The Roundup Gang had spent years in a storage box as Al searched for Woody.

"Woo-eee!" howled Jessie. **"Look at us! Now we're a complete set!"**

Then Woody, Jessie, and Bullseye started playing with the Roundup toys.

"Now Al can sell us to the museum in Japan," said the Prospector.

"Museum?" asked Woody. "But I've gotta get back home to my owner, Andy."

Jessie was crushed. Without Woody, they would be returned to the storage box.

When Al returned, the toys heard him telephone the toy museum in Japan. **The museum agreed to buy the Roundup Gang!**

Al called a man to come and spruce up Woody. Soon the cowboy was not just good as new—he was even better than new. The man even painted over Andy's name on the bottom of Woody's shoe.

But it didn't matter. Woody was still ready to go back home to Andy. Then, Jessie told him about her little girl.

"Andy's your best friend, right?" Jessie asked. "When he plays with you, you feel alive."

"How did you know that?" asked Woody.

"Because my owner, Emily, was just the same. She was my whole world," Jessie told him. "She gave me away when she grew up."

Jessie's words made Woody wonder if he should stay with the Roundup Gang instead of going home.

In the meantime, the other toys had reached Al's Toy Barn. They stood across the street from the toy store. But to cross the busy road, they had to hide in traffic cones!

Soon they were all safe on the other side.

Buzz and the gang slipped inside Al's Toy Barn. They didn't find Woody, but they did meet some interesting toys and they discovered Al's address!

At last **the toys went to Al's apartment and found their missing buddy.**

"Woody!" Buzz cried. "You're in danger here. We need to leave."

But Woody didn't want to go. He told his friends about the TV show, the Roundup Gang, and the museum. "Andy is growing up, and one day he won't need me any longer. This is my chance to last forever in a museum," Woody explained.

"Museum? You want to watch children from behind glass? Some life!" Buzz wailed. "You are a toy, Woody. **You have to be there for Andy.** Remember? You taught me that."

But Woody wouldn't go.

As the other toys from Andy's room sadly left the apartment, Woody turned and saw his old TV show. On the TV set was a boy who looked like Andy. Woody scratched off the paint from his shoe and looked at Andy's name. He knew he'd made a mistake.

"What am I doing?!" Woody shouted.

So what if someday Andy outgrew him? he thought. Until then, **Woody wanted to spend every single minute with his best friend.**

"Buzz! Buzz! Wait!" Woody called out. "I'm coming with you!"

Woody asked Jessie and Bullseye to come, too.

But the Prospector slipped out of his box and stopped them. "I've waited too long for this!" he yelled. "You are not going to ruin my plans!"

Before they could get any further, **Al came in!**

Al grabbed the Roundup Gang and put them in a case. He was heading for the airport to fly to Japan. There he would sell them to the museum.

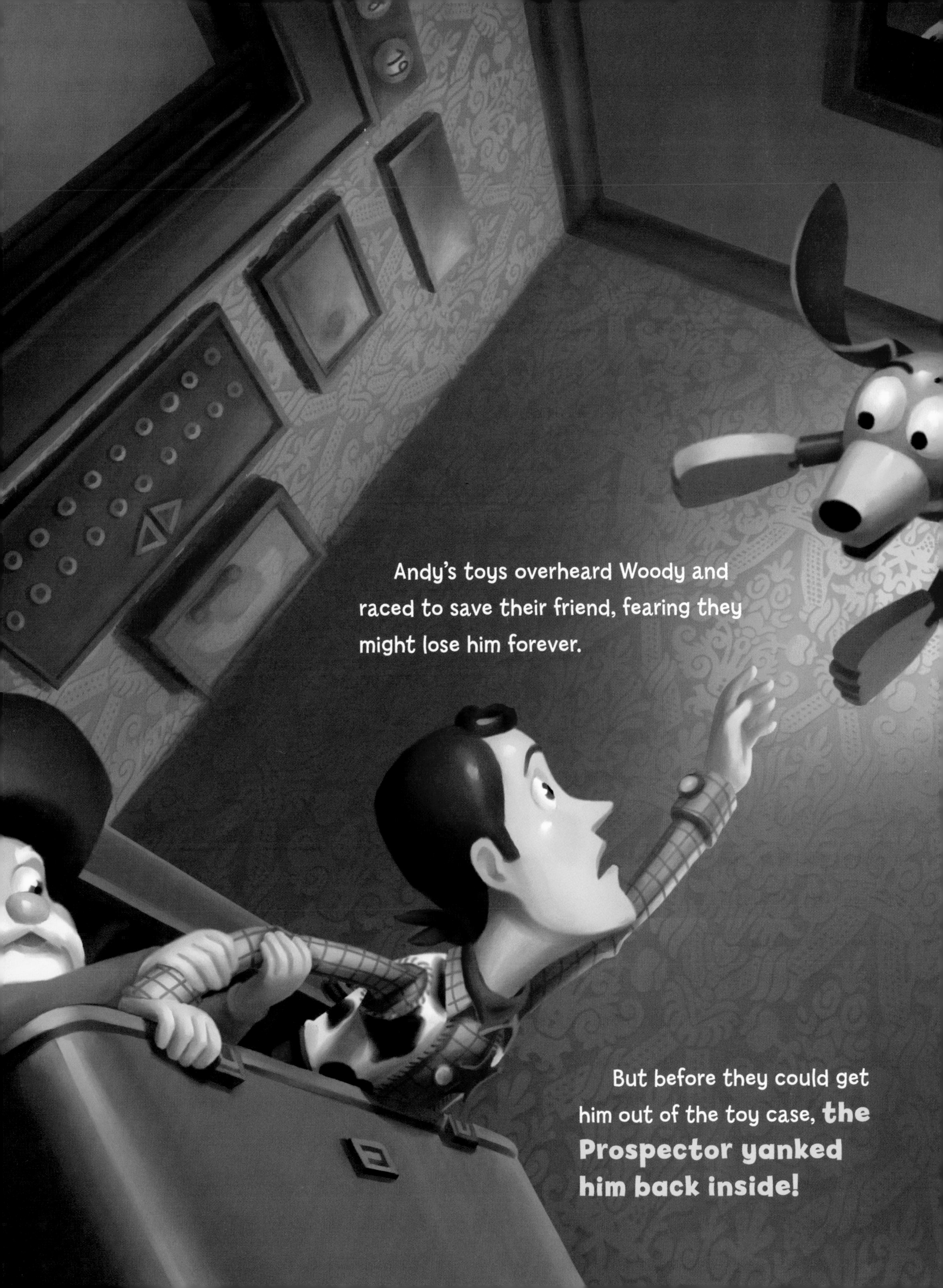

Andy's toys overheard Woody and raced to save their friend, fearing they might lose him forever.

But before they could get him out of the toy case, **the Prospector yanked him back inside!**

Buzz and the gang ran outside after Al. But Al got into his car and sped off.

"How are we going to get Woody now?" Rex asked.

Just then, the toys spotted a Pizza Planet delivery van. The toys jumped into the vehicle.

"Slink, take the pedals!" Buzz commanded. "Rex, you navigate. Hamm, you operate the levers and knobs!"

They raced after Al's car.

When Al reached the airport, he had to check in the toy case. Then it went into the baggage area on a conveyor belt that took the bags out to the planes.

The Roundup Gang was on its way to Japan!

But Buzz and the other toys, hiding in a pet carrier, followed the case into the baggage area. Buzz set out to rescue his friend.

Buzz, Woody, and Bullseye managed to escape, but Jessie was still trapped in Al's case.

"Woody! Help!" pleaded Jessie as she was loaded onto the plane.

Then Woody jumped aboard the plane.

"Come on, Jessie!" urged Woody. **"It's time to take you home."**

"But I'm a girl toy," Jessie moaned. "Andy's not gonna like me."

"Nonsense!" Woody replied. "Andy'll love you!"

Suddenly, the baggage door closed. The plane started to move! There was only one way out—an opening just above the landing gear. Woody led the way.

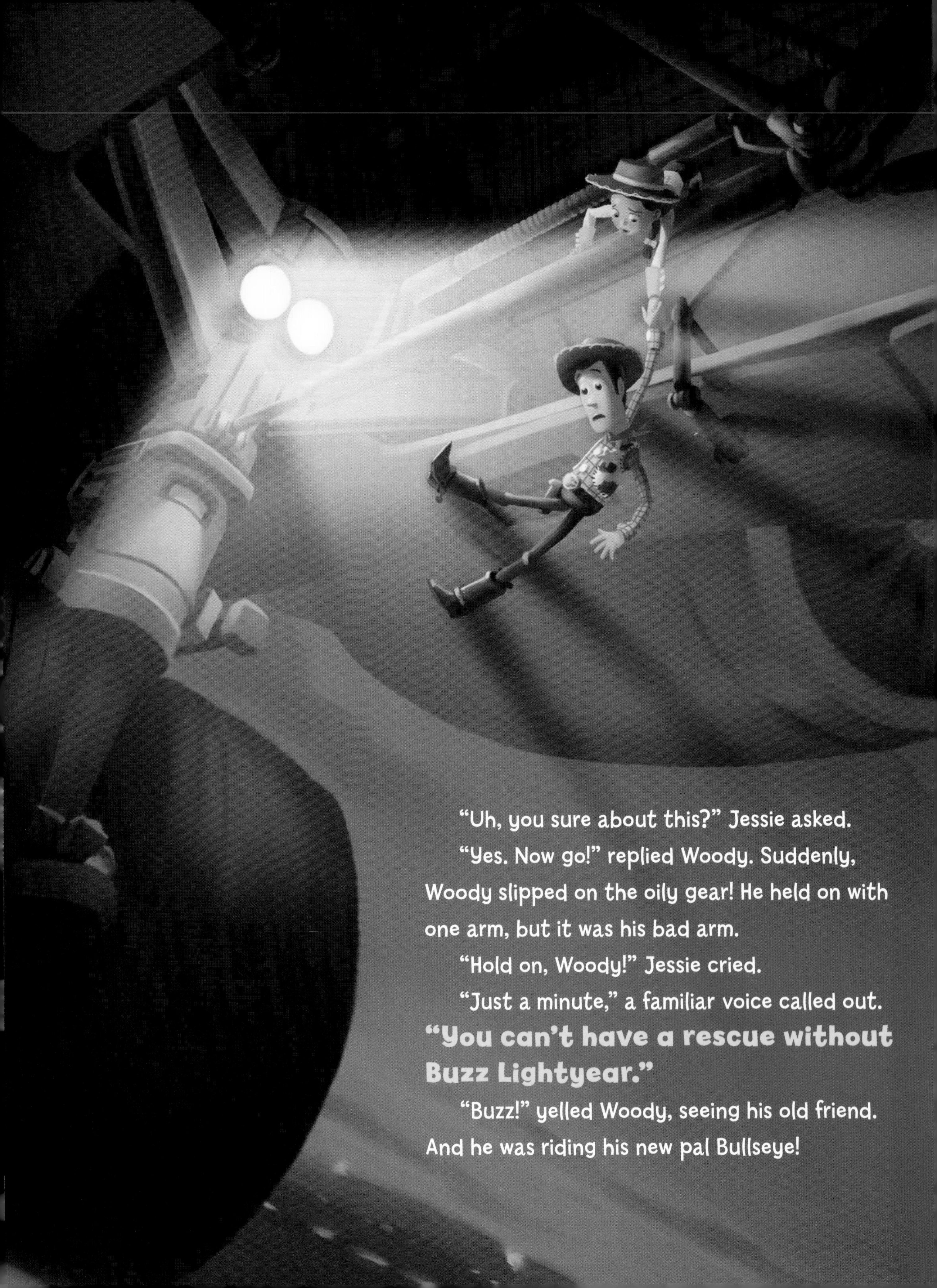

"Uh, you sure about this?" Jessie asked.

"Yes. Now go!" replied Woody. Suddenly, Woody slipped on the oily gear! He held on with one arm, but it was his bad arm.

"Hold on, Woody!" Jessie cried.

"Just a minute," a familiar voice called out. **"You can't have a rescue without Buzz Lightyear."**

"Buzz!" yelled Woody, seeing his old friend. And he was riding his new pal Bullseye!

Then Woody had an idea. He twirled his pull string like a lasso and wrapped it around the landing gear. Woody and Jessie swung down and landed safely on Bullseye.

"Now, let's all go home," Woody said, grinning.

And what happened to the Prospector? In the airport, Woody and Buzz had strapped him to a pink backpack, and pushed him into the baggage return. On the other side was an excited little girl who couldn't wait to play with a new doll. **The Prospector wouldn't be in perfect condition much longer!**

When Andy came back from camp, he bounded up the stairs to his room, where he saw Woody and Buzz and his brand-new Jessie and Bullseye toys.

"Oh, wow! Thanks!" he called downstairs to his mother.

Someday, Andy would grow up, and maybe he wouldn't always play with toys. But Woody and Buzz knew there was no place they'd rather be. Besides, **they'd always have each other—for infinity and beyond!**

At Kohl's, we believe the simple act of caring creates a sense of community. Thanks to people like you, over the past 10 years Kohl's Cares for Kids® has raised millions of dollars to support children in the communities we serve. Throughout the year, Kohl's sells special Kohl's Cares for Kids merchandise with 100% of the net profit benefiting children's health and education initiatives nationwide.

Kohl's Cares for Kids is our way of supporting our customers and improving children's lives. So when you turn the pages of this book, remember you're not only reading a fun-filled adventure, you're also helping make a difference in the life of a child.

For more information about Kohl's Cares for Kids programs, visit www.kohlscorporation.com.

For information address Disney Press, 114 Fifth Avenue, New York, New York 10011-5690.

Printed in the United States of America

First Edition

1 3 5 7 9 10 8 6 4 2

Library of Congress Catalog Card Number on file.

ISBN 978-1-4231-2790-1
ISBN 978-1-4231-3750-4
G942-9090-6-10046

For more Disney Press fun, visit www.disneybooks.com

PWC-SFICOC-260
FOR TEXT ONLY